Monster on the Loose

A MONSTER AT SCHOOL

By Amanda Huneke

Illustrated by
Guy Wolek

magic Wagon

visit us at www.abdopublishing.com

Published by Magic Wagon, a division of the ABDO Group, PO Box 398166, Minneapolis, MN 55439.
Copyright © 2013 by Abdo Consulting Group, Inc. International copyrights reserved in all countries. All rights
reserved. No part of this book may be reproduced in any form without written permission from the publisher.

Looking Glass Library™ is a trademark and logo of Magic Wagon.

Printed in the United States of America, North Mankato, Minnesota.
102012
012013
♻ This book contains at least 10% recycled materials.

Written by Amanda Huneke
Illustrations by Guy Wolek
Edited by Stephanie Hedlund and Rochelle Baltzer
Cover and interior design by Neil Klinepier

Library of Congress Cataloging-in-Publication Data

Huneke, Amanda, 1985-
  A monster at school / by Amanda Huneke ; illustrated by Guy Wolek.
    p. cm. -- (Monster on the loose)
  Summary: When she hears strange, loud noises coming from her brother's kindergarten room, a young girl becomes
convinced that there is a monster loose in the school.
  ISBN 978-1-61641-931-8
  1. Monsters--Juvenile fiction. 2. Kindergarten--Juvenile fiction. 3. Elementary schools--Juvenile fiction. 4.
Brothers and sisters--Juvenile fiction. 5. Imagination--Juvenile fiction. [1. Monsters--Fiction. 2. Kindergarten-
-Fiction. 3. Elementary schools--Fiction. 4. Schools--Fiction. 5. Brothers and sisters--Fiction. 6. Imagination--
Fiction.] I. Wolek, Guy, ill. II. Title.
  PZ7.H8997Mon 2013
  813.6--dc23   2012028616

It's noisy! It's loud!
So many sounds fill my ears!

What's that **rumbling**?
Who's that grumbling?

What's going
on here?

Strange noises and voices echo off the wall.
I wonder what waits at the end of the hall.

When quiet settles,

I creep on ahead,

past door after door
until the hallway's end.

I listen closely, my ear to the door.

Until suddenly, the room's booming with hoots, SHRIEKS, and ROARS!

It's so rowdy and wild,
it sounds like a zoo!

But, what if . . . oh no . . .

. . . there's a monster at school?

I stretch up on tiptoe to peek through the window . . .

. . . but crouch back down at another loud **bellow!**

I freeze at once, afraid of what's inside.
As I wonder how many monsters I will find.

I reach for the doorknob
and give a slight turn,
keeping quiet and secret
so I can sneak in unheard.

I inch the door forward
and lean to peek inside,
just as another monster rushes by!

I reach up again to give it another try.
I open the door all the way, and . . .

. . . I can't believe my eyes!

It's nothing like I imagined from out in the hall.

It's filled with laughter and smiles, fun and delight.
And most surprising of all . . .

...no monsters in sight!

No monsters? Not one? But how can that be?

I look under desks and behind backpacks, but none do I see!

Instead, behind all the books, blocks, and clay,
it's not monsters—but children—that are busy at play.

In here, the ones making noise
are my little brother's class of
girls and boys.

GLOSSARY

bellow - to make a deep, loud roar like a bull.

crouch - to lower the body close to the ground by bending the legs.

echo - sounds bouncing off a surface and repeating.

grumbling - making deep, angry, quiet sounds; rumbling.

rowdy - rough or loud behavior.

shriek - a cry in a loud, high-pitched voice.

sneak - to move about in a sly or secret way.

stretch - to reach out.

tiptoe - to walk on the tips of one's toes.

About the Author:
Amanda Huneke is a writer, military wife, and mother. She and her husband grew up in the small farming community of Goodhue, Minnesota, where they were never lacking in adventures (thankfully, not too many involved monsters). Amanda has her son and daughter to thank for the inspiration they provided for her first picture book series; and, like the Monster books, for the adventures they create every day.

About the Illustrator:
Guy Wolek started illustrating in the 1980s doing dark, moody paintings. In 1995, his wife, Debi, encouraged him to do children's art since he had always drawn humorous characters and scenes for fun. Now as a children's book illustrator he has the opportunity to do something he enjoys every day.

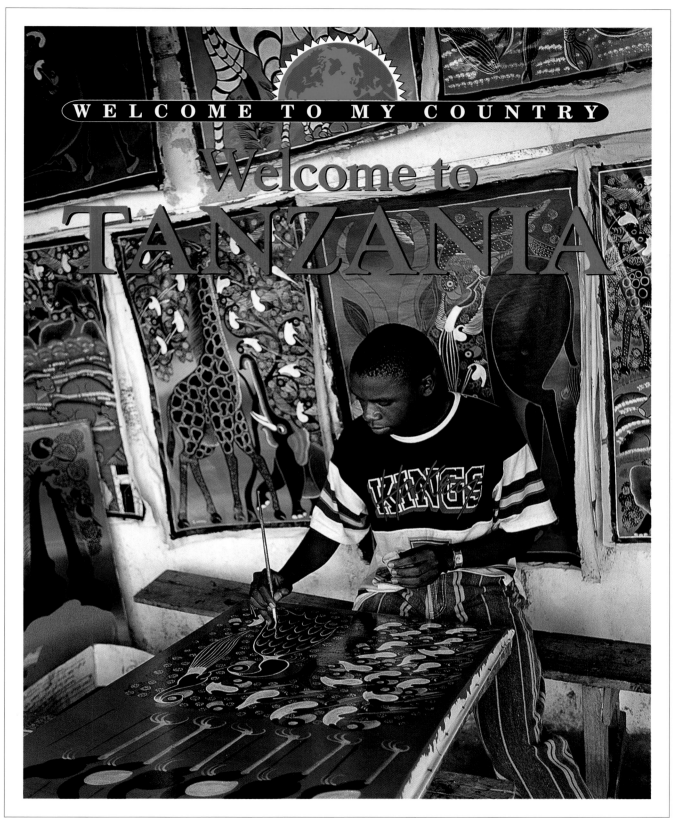

Welcome to
TANZANIA

Gareth Stevens Publishing
A WORLD ALMANAC EDUCATION GROUP COMPANY

Written by
CHIN OI LING

Edited by
KATHARINE BROWN-CARPENTER

Edited in USA by
JENETTE DONOVAN GUNTLY

Designed by
BENSON TAN

Picture research by
THOMAS KHOO
JOSHUA ANG

First published in North America in 2006 by
Gareth Stevens Publishing
A WRC Media Company
330 West Olive Street, Suite 100
Milwaukee, Wisconsin 53212 USA

Please visit our web site at
www.garethstevens.com
For a free color catalog describing
Gareth Stevens Publishing's list of high-quality
books and multimedia programs,
call 1-800-542-2595 (USA) or
1-800-387-3178 (Canada).
Gareth Stevens Publishing's fax: (414) 332-3567.

© **MARSHALL CAVENDISH INTERNATIONAL (ASIA)**
PRIVATE LIMITED 2005
Originated and designed by
Times Editions—Marshall Cavendish
An imprint of Marshall Cavendish International (Asia) Pte Ltd
A member of Times Publishing Limited
Times Centre, 1 New Industrial Road
Singapore 536196
http://www.marshallcavendish.com/genref

Library of Congress Cataloging-in-Publication Data
Chin, Oi Ling.
Welcome to Tanzania / Chin Oi Ling.
p. cm. — (Welcome to my country)
Includes bibliographical references and index.
ISBN 0-8368-3137-3 (lib. bdg.)
1. Tanzania — Juvenile literature. I. Title. II. Series.
DT438.C56   2005
967.8—dc22   2004065305

Printed in Singapore

1 2 3 4 5 6 7 8 9 09 08 07 06 05

PICTURE CREDITS
Agence France Presse: 15 (bottom), 16,
    17, 36 (bottom), 37
Art Directors & TRIP Photo Library:
    3 (bottom), 9 (top), 28
Corbis: 38
David Cumming/Eye Ubiquitous: 1, 3 (top),
    12 (bottom), 45
Focus Team—Italy: 3 (center), 4,
    19 (bottom), 27, 33, 34
David Forman/Eye Ubiquitous: 8
HBL Network: cover, 2, 12 (top), 18, 22, 26,
    32, 35
The Hutchison Library: 6, 14, 15 (top), 23,
    25, 40
Laure Communications: 10, 11, 20
Lonely Planet Images: 29
James Mollison/Eye Ubiquitous: 36 (top)
Bob Pateman: 7 (top), 21, 41
Mike Powles/Eye Ubiqitous: 9 (bottom), 43
Audrius Tomonis – www.banknotes.com:
    44 (both)
Topham Picturepoint: 30, 39
Travel Ink: 7 (bottom), 13, 19 (top)
A. van Zandbergen/AfriPics: 31
Nik Wheeler: 5, 24

Digital Scanning by Superskill Graphics Pte Ltd

Contents

Words that appear in the glossary are printed in **boldface** type the first time they occur in the text.

Welcome to Tanzania!

In 1964, the Republic of Tanganyika and the Republic of Zanzibar became one nation, the United Republic of Tanzania. The country is located in East Africa and is famous for its wild Serengeti region and for grand Mount Kilimanjaro. Let's explore Tanzania and learn about its interesting people!

The Flag of Tanzania

On Tanzania's flag, the green triangle stands for the land. The black stripe stretching from corner to corner stands for Tanzania's people. The yellow bands are for the country's wealth of minerals. The blue triangle is for the sea.

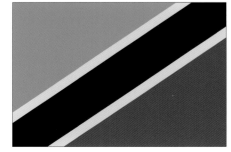

The Land

Tanzania has an area of 364,900 square miles (945,087 square kilometers). Land surrounds the country to the north, south, and west. To the east is the Indian Ocean. The islands of Mafia, Pemba, and Zanzibar are also part of Tanzania.

The Western Rift Valley runs along Tanzania's western border. The Eastern Rift Valley runs through the central part of the country. In between is the Central **Plateau**. It covers one-third of the land.

Opposite: The Great Ruaha River joins the Rufiji River and flows eastward into the Indian Ocean.

Below: Many types of animals and plants live in the Ngorongoro **Conservation** Area, which is part of the Serengeti region.

Tanzania has many mountain ranges. Mount Kilimanjaro in the northeastern part of the country is the highest mountain in Africa. It is 19,340 feet (5,895 meters) high.

Lake Victoria, which borders Kenya and Uganda, is the second-largest freshwater lake in the world. Lake Tanganyika in the west is the world's second-deepest lake. Tanzania also has several major rivers, including the Pangani, Rufiji, Ruvuma, and Wami.

Below: Mount Kilimanjaro has three peaks. The highest peak is known as Kibo (*below*). Kibo is always covered with snow.

Climate

Tanzania's climate is mainly **tropical**, but the country does have a hot and a cold season. The hot season is from November to February. Temperatures in most parts of Tanzania, including the islands, range from about 77° to 86° Fahrenheit (25° to 30° Celsius) in the hot season. The cold season is from May to August. Temperatures in the cold season range from 59° to 68° F (15° to 20° C). The highland areas are cooler than the rest of the land all year.

Below: The Great Ruaha River often runs low during the dry season. Nearly half of the country receives less than 30 inches (750 millimeters) of rain each year.

Plants and Animals

Many kinds of plants grow in Tanzania. The Serengeti National Park consists mostly of **savannas**, with some forests and marshes. Many unusual plants grow in the park, including strangle fig trees, sausage trees, and toothbrush trees.

Many animals, such as lions, zebras, giraffes, and elephants, live in Tanzania. Almost five hundred kinds of birds, including ostriches, live in the country.

9

History

People have lived in what are now the northern and central parts of Tanzania for thousands of years. Arabs were the first visitors to arrive. They explored the coast and central regions of the land in search of trade routes and slaves to trade. Portuguese explorers arrived in the 1400s. They gained power over the Arabs by taking control of the coast. In the 1700s, **native** groups and the Arabs drove the Portuguese out of the area.

Below: The Old Fort was built by the Arabs in 1700. They used it to defend themselves from Portuguese attacks. Today, the fort is a **cultural** center.

Left: Julius Nyerere (*right*) gives his first speech as prime minister of newly independent Tanganyika in 1961. In 1954, he founded a political party, the Tanganyika African National Union (TANU), which grew to be very powerful.

The British arrived in the region in the 1840s. The Germans arrived in the 1880s. In 1886, the two countries split East Africa. The Germans took over the area that became known as Tanganyika.

In 1919, after World War I, Britain took over. The **United Nations** (UN) took control in 1947. Britain was put in charge of helping Tanganyika set up a new government. In 1959, Britain supported a plan to make Tanganyika independent. The country became fully independent from Britain in 1961.

Zanzibar's Early Days

Native groups from the continent of Africa were the first people to live on the island of Zanzibar. From the 600s to the 900s A.D., Arabs and groups of people from Persia settled on Zanzibar. The Arabs and Persians married some native people. Their **descendants** were known as Shirazis or Swahilis.

Beginning in 1503, the Portuguese forced the people of Zanzibar to pay a **tribute** each year. In 1698, the Arabs forced the Portuguese out of Zanzibar.

Above: Under the rule of Seyyid Said bin Sultan, an Arab, Zanzibar grew to be an important center of trade, especially in slaves.

Below: Some of the walls of Fukuchani, better known as the Portuguese House, still stand today.

Above:
This building is in Stone Town on the island of Zanzibar. It used to serve as the headquarters of the island's political parties.

In 1890, the British took control of Zanzibar. A **sultan** still ruled the island, but all of his rulings had to be approved by the British. In 1913, the British took full control of the island.

In 1960, the British approved a new **constitution** for Zanzibar. Political parties formed. In December 1963, the country became independent. A sultan took over, but a month later, Africans on Zanzibar took control of the country. They chose Abeid Kurame as president.

Tanganyika and Zanzibar Join

In April 1964, Tanganyika joined with Zanzibar to form the United Republic of Tanganyika and Zanzibar. In October 1964, the nation's name was changed to the United Republic of Tanzania. Julius Nyerere was **executive** president, and Abeid Kurame was first vice president.

In 1972, Kurame was killed. Nyerere served as president until 1985, when he left office and Ali Hassan Mwinyi took over. In 1995 and 2000, Benjamin William Mkapa was elected president.

Left: Before 1964, Julius Nyerere (*right*) served as the leader of Tanganyika. Abeid Kurame (*left*) was Zanzibar's leader. After the countries joined, the balance of power between the two lands was kept equal by giving both men positions in the government.

Mirambo (1840–1884)

Mirambo was a **warlord** from central Africa. He brought native Nyamwezi groups together and formed a kingdom strong enough to keep the Arabs from taking over central Tanganyika.

Julius Kambarage Nyerere (1922–1999)

Julius Kambarage Nyerere

Julius Kambarage Nyerere was the first Tanganyikan to be educated in Britain. He served as Tanganyika's first prime minister. From 1962 to 1985, Nyerere served as president of Tanganyika and then Tanzania. He worked to improve farming and also made laws to improve education and health care.

Benjamin William Mkapa (1938–)

Benjamin William Mkapa

As president of Tanzania since 1995, Benjamin William Mkapa has strongly supported trade and **democracy**. He has fought for the rights of Tanzanians and has also fought poverty in the country.

Government and the Economy

The Tanzanian government has three branches. The executive branch, which is headed by the president, makes rules for the government and also runs it. The president chooses a prime minister and a cabinet, which is a group of advisers. Tanzania's legislative, or lawmaking, branch is the National Assembly, which is a **parliament**. The judiciary branch includes primary courts, district courts, high courts, and the Court of **Appeal**.

Left: Some voters in Tanzania fill out ballots during the elections of 2000. During that election, Benjamin Mkapa was elected to a second five-year term as president.

In addition to Tanzania's government officials, Zanzibar elects some of its own officials as well. The island elects its own president, who makes decisions only for Zanzibar. The Zanzibar House of Representatives makes its own laws. The island has its own high courts, too.

Tanzania's **mainland** is divided into twenty-one government regions. The islands are divided into five regions. Each region is divided into districts.

Above: Supporters of Benjamin Mkapa and the Chama Cha Mapinduzi (CCM) political party cheer in the streets.

The Economy

Tanzania is one of the poorest countries in the world. More than one-third of all Tanzanians live in poverty.

Some Tanzanians work in service jobs or in industries. Most industries in Tanzania make products from crops. For example, sisal plants are made into sisal twine, which is a strong type of string. Other goods produced include cement, salt, shoes, cloth, and paper.

Below: In Tanzania, many of the goods that are **exported** to other countries are moved on trains.

Farming and Mining

In 2002, most Tanzanians worked in farming. Crops grown in the country include coffee, cotton, cashew nuts, tea, and tobacco. Other crops include corn, bananas, **cassavas**, and rice. Most crops grown in Tanzania are exported.

Mining is an important industry in Tanzania. Tanzanians mine coal, gold, and tin as well as diamonds and other gemstones. The country is famous for tanzanite, a rare blue-purple gemstone that is found only in Tanzania.

Above: Zanzibar is famous for the spices it exports, including nutmeg (*shown*). Cloves and other spices are also grown on the island.

People and Lifestyle

Tanzania has more than 120 different **ethnic** groups. Most groups are made up of descendants of the Bantu people, including Tanzania's largest groups, the Nyamwezi and the Sukuma.

Almost all people living in mainland Tanzania are native Africans. Small numbers of Arabs, Europeans, and Asians also live on the mainland. On Zanzibar, almost everyone is Arab or native African or a mixture of the two.

Left:
Most people in Tanzania are fairly young. Almost half of all Tanzanians are fourteen years old or younger.

Country Life and City Life

Most people in Tanzania live in the countryside and make a living by farming. Growing crops is difficult for many Tanzanian farmers. Over time, as more and more people set up farms and grew crops, the land became less **fertile**. The farmers could not grow as many plants, and harvests were poor.

Some Tanzanians live in cities. The country's largest city is Dar es Salaam. Other cities include Arusha, Mbeya, Mwanza, and the city of Zanzibar.

Above: These two Maasai women sit outside in a city. Many people from Tanzania's native groups, such as the Maasai, have moved to cities from the countryside to find better ways of life.

Family Life

Tanzanians have strong family ties to their parents and other family members. Many important life events, including marriages and births, are celebrated by large family groups. They usually hold **traditional** ceremonies to celebrate.

In the countryside, most Tanzanian men hunt and herd for work. Women usually do chores and tend crops. Most families include many children, who are expected to help farm and herd animals.

Below: In Tanzania, older children are expected to help take care of their younger brothers and sisters.

In Tanzania, many marriages are arranged by friends or family members. Many Tanzanian girls marry while they are still in their early teens.

Above: Women and children wait for medical care. In 1975, Tanzania started a program to improve health care. Still, many babies die in the country each year.

Health Problems

Most Tanzanian men only live about forty-three years. Most women only live about forty-six years. Many people in Tanzania die of diseases. The worst disease in the country is malaria. Many Tanzanians also die of AIDS, sleeping sickness, or pneumonia.

Education

School in Tanzania is divided into three levels. All children must receive basic schooling. Basic schooling includes two years of preprimary school and seven years of primary school. After primary school, students may choose to receive a secondary education, which includes four years of junior secondary school and then two years of senior secondary school. Subjects studied in secondary school include farming and science.

Many secondary school classes teach skills used in everyday life. To find out what it is like to live in the countryside, secondary school students from cities are expected to work in nearby villages.

Higher Education

After secondary school, students may choose to attend a university, college, or **vocational** school. Tanzania also has adult classes in subjects such as crafts, farming, and mathematics.

Left: Because all boys and girls are required to attend primary school in Tanzania, more people in that country can read and write than in most other nations in Africa.

Religion

Almost all people on Tanzania's islands are Muslims, followers of the Islamic religion. The Arabs first brought Islam with them to Zanzibar, where they went to build trading posts. Islam then spread to the mainland. Today, about one-third of mainland Tanzanians are Muslim.

About one-third of Tanzanians on the mainland are Christian. The two largest Christian groups in the country are the Lutherans and the Roman Catholics.

Below: A man sits to read in a mosque, which is an Islamic house of worship. All mosques have separate areas for men and women.

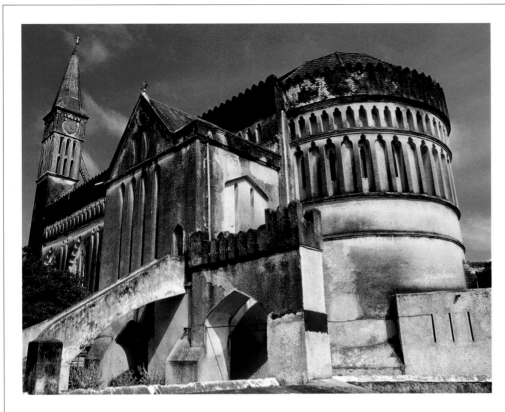

Left: The Church of Christ is in the city of Zanzibar. It was built in the 1870s. The church was built on the place where the old slave market used to be.

The Portuguese brought the Christian religion to the region when they set up **missions**. Later, the British set up more Christian missions in the country.

Tanzania has many native religions. Some of the religions include a belief in the spirits of **ancestors**. Many people in the countryside practice a mixture of native and Islamic or Christian beliefs.

Some Asian Tanzanians practice the Sikh, Buddhist, or Hindu religions. A few people practice the Baha'i faith.

Language

The Tanzanians have more than eighty-seven languages. Swahili and English are the country's official languages. Swahili is used in the government and during the first seven years of school. It is a Bantu language that includes many Arabic words. English is used in higher education and for trade. Many people, especially in Zanzibar, speak Arabic as well. Others speak local languages.

Below: The words painted on this wall are written in both Swahili and English.

Literature

In the past, stories in Tanzania were not written down. They were told out loud and were passed from one generation to the next in that way. Printed literature began in the nation in the 1930s. One famous Tanzanian author was Shaaban Robert (1909–1962). He supported the Swahili culture and African traditions of telling stories aloud. Today, famous Tanzanian authors include Tololwa Mollel and Euphrase Kezilahabi.

Arts

Music and Instruments

Tanzanians enjoy many kinds of music. In Zanzibar, *taarab* (taa-RAB) is a popular kind of music in which poems are sung. Some kinds of jazz and the *mtindo* (mu-EEN-doh), a type of dance music, are also popular in Tanzania. Important instruments include many kinds of drums and the *marimba* (mah-RIM-bah), which is a finger piano.

Below: This man is playing at the Dar es Salaam Music and Dance Festival. It is a contest in which people from mainland Tanzania perform ethnic music and dances.

Above:
These Maasai
are performing
a dance in which
they jump up and
down. Dance is an
important part of
life for the ethnic
groups of Tanzania.

Dance

In Tanzania, dancing is important. The *ngoma* (ng-OH-mah) is a style of dance and music used to show everyday life and to celebrate special events. Dances such as the *chakacha* (chah-KAH-chah) and the *lelemama* (LEH-leh-MAH-mah) are only performed by women.

Most native groups in Tanzania have their own dance traditions. The Sukuma hold live snakes while they dance. The Maasai leap into the air and chant.

Crafts

Tanzania's native groups make many kinds of crafts. The Makonde are well known for their wood carvings. They make beautiful masks and small statues, mostly out of ebony, a very dark wood.

The Maasai are well known for the designs they carve on their shields and spears. They are also famous for the colorful beaded collars they make for ceremonies. The Maasai use beads even on everyday objects, making the items into beautiful works of art.

Above:
These two men in the countryside of Zanzibar are weaving baskets out of coconut leaves. In Tanzania, baskets are woven in many shapes and bright colors.

Another popular craft in Tanzania is making clay pots. Today, clay pots are made in the same way they were made about one thousand years ago. Some of the longest-lasting pots are made from clay found on Mount Kilimanjaro and the Pare Mountains. Elderly women in villages make the most beautiful pots.

Zanzibar is famous for doors carved with fancy designs. Many designs are carved in Arabic art styles. Today, there are about 560 carved doors in Zanzibar.

Below: This man is looking at a model of a *dhow* (DA-ow). Dhows are common boats in Tanzania, and model dhows are often created to sell as souvenirs.

Leisure

Many Tanzanians like to spend their leisure time with family and friends. Singing, dancing, playing games, and sports are also popular activities.

Storytelling is very popular in the country. The stories are told for fun, but they are also told to teach children the rules of society and to explain values that are important to their culture. Some popular stories explain nature, such as why two of Mount Kilimanjaro's peaks, Kibo and Mawenzi, look so different.

Left: Tanzanians spend most of their free time visiting family or friends. They often gather in homes or meet at roadside stands to talk.

Bao

Many Tanzanians enjoy playing a game called *bao* (BA-ow). Bao is played on a board with four rows of eight pits each. Each player has two rows of pits and a pile of seeds. The players fill some pits in the front rows with seeds. On each turn, a player puts a seed into one pit in the front row. The move lets the player claim seeds in the other player's pit in the next row up. At the end, the player with the most seeds wins.

Above: Tanzanian boys play a game of bao. Bao is believed to be about three thousand years old. It is played in many ways in countries in Africa and Asia.

Sports

Tanzanians enjoy playing many sports. Soccer is one of the most popular sports in the country, and children often play it using a ball made out of plastic bags.

Above: This young Tanzanian boy is playing with a soccer ball made from plastic bags.

Tanzanian women and girls like to play netball, which is similar to basketball. Players must keep at least one foot on the ground when they hold the ball. They cannot dribble or hold the ball for more than three seconds.

Left: The Taifa Stars, Tanzania's national soccer team, has played in international competitions such as the African Cup of Nations.

Running is another favorite sport in Tanzania. Each year, the country holds a marathon to look for good runners. Famous Tanzanian runners John Yuda, Francis Naali, and Filbert Bayi all won medals at the Commonwealth Games.

Boxing is also popular in Tanzania. Rashid Matumla became famous in 1998 as the first Tanzanian to win the World Boxing Union title for the light-middleweight category.

Above: In the 1998 Commonwealth Games, Tanzania's Michael Yomba (*left*) fought against Clied Musonda (*right*), of Zimbabwe. Yomba won the match and later went on to win a gold medal.

Festivals and Holidays

Muslim festivals are very important in Tanzania. The Muslim festival of *Idd-El-Fitr* (EED-al-FIT-er) marks the end of **Ramadan**. Muslims celebrate Idd-El-Fitr by holding feasts and by buying and wearing new clothes. During the festival of *Idd-El-Hajj* (EED-al-HAJ), some Muslim Tanzanians go on **pilgrimages** to Mecca in Saudi Arabia.

Above: This group of Hindus living on the island of Zanzibar gathered to celebrate the birthday of Krishna, one of the most important gods in the Hindu religion.

Christmas is an important holiday for Tanzanian Christians. On that day, they go to church, exchange presents, and spend time with their families.

Tanzania also has national holidays. December 9 is Independence Day. It marks independence from Britain and is celebrated throughout the country. Every year, Zanzibar holds the Festival of Dhow Countries. It includes dhow races and art and cultural events.

Below: On July 7, Tanzanians across the nation celebrate Saba Saba. The day marks the founding of the Tanganyika African National Union (TANU), the political party that was started by Julius Nyerere.

Food

The main food in most of Tanzania is *ugali* (u-GAH-lih), a thick porridge made of cassava, cornmeal, **sorghum**, or a grain called millet. Ugali is usually eaten with meat, stew, or vegetables. In coastal regions, the main food is pilaf, which is rice cooked with spices.

Mishikaki (mih-shih-KAH-kih), or meat grilled over a fire, is a favorite Tanzanian dish. Seafood is popular in coastal areas and near lakes and rivers.

Left: These women in the city of Arusha are preparing dough to bake bread.

Many mainland Tanzanians enjoy hot tea. Sugar cane juice is a favorite drink among Tanzanians in Zanzibar.

Tanzanians usually eat with their hands. At the start and end of each meal, they wash their hands in bowls of water that are passed around. Food is often served in one big bowl. Diners use their right hands to take food from the bowls and to eat the food. They only use their left hands to handle hard-to-hold food such as meat with bones.

Above: On the island of Zanzibar, fruit markets are common. Often, Tanzanians eat fruit for dessert.

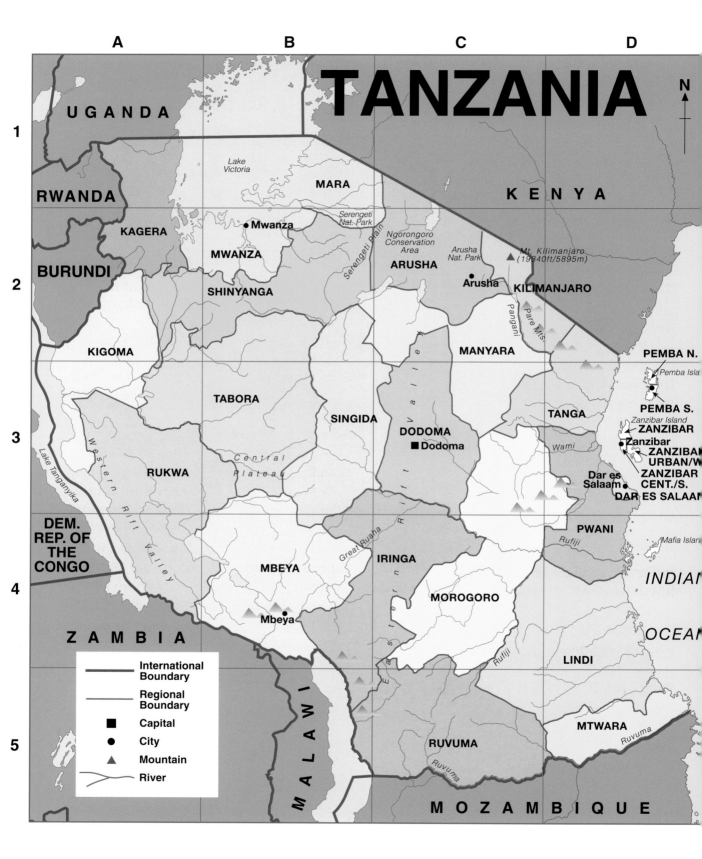

TANZANIA

N

Arusha (city) C2
Arusha (region) C1–D3
Arusha National Park C2

Burundi A2

Central Plateau B3

Dar es Salaam (city) D3
Dar es Salaam (region) D3
Democratic Republic of the Congo A3–A4
Dodoma (city) C3
Dodoma (region) C2–D4

Eastern Rift Valley C2–C5

Great Ruaha River B4–C3

Indian Ocean D2–D5
Iringa (region) B3–C5

Kagera (region) A1–A2
Kenya B1–D2
Kigoma (region) A2–A3
Kilimanjaro (region) C2–D2

Lake Tanganyika A2–A4

Lake Victoria A1–B2
Lindi (region) C4–D5

Mafia Island D4
Malawi B4–B5
Manyara (region) C2–D3
Mara (region) B1–C2
Mbeya (city) B4
Mbeya (region) B4
Morogoro (region) C3–D4
Mount Kilimanjaro C2
Mozambique B5–D5
Mtwara (region) D5
Mwanza (city) B2
Mwanza (region) A2–B2

Ngorongoro Conservation Area C2

Pangani River C2–D3
Pare Mountains C2
Pemba Island D3
Pemba North (region) D3
Pemba South (region) D3
Pwani (region) C3–D4

Rufiji River C4–D4
Rukwa (region) A3–B4
Ruvuma (region) B5–D5

Above: Cheetahs are just one of the many animals that live in the Serengeti region.

Ruvuma River C5–D5
Rwanda A1–A2

Serengeti B2–C2
Serengeti National Park B1–B2
Shinyanga (region) A2–B2
Singida (region) B2–C3

Tabora (region) A2–B3
Tanga (region) C3–D3

Uganda A1–B1

Wami River C3–D3
Western Rift Valley A3–A4

Zambia A4–B5
Zanzibar (city) D3
Zanzibar Central/ South (region) D3
Zanzibar Island D3
Zanzibar North (region) D3
Zanzibar Urban/ West (region) D3

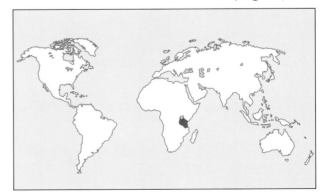

Quick Facts

Official Name   United Republic of Tanzania

Capital   Dodoma

Official Languages   English, Swahili

Population   36,588,225 (July 2004 estimate)

Land Area   364,900 square miles (945,087 sq km)

Regions   Arusha, Dar es Salaam, Dodoma, Iringa, Kagera, Kigoma, Kilimanjaro, Lindi, Manyara, Mara, Mbeya, Morogoro, Mtwara, Mwanza, Pemba North, Pemba South, Pwani, Rukwa, Ruvuma, Shinyanga, Singida, Tabora, Tanga, Zanzibar Central/South, Zanzibar North, Zanzibar Urban/West

Highest Point   Mount Kilimanjaro 19,340 feet (5,895 m)

Main Religions   Christianity, Islam, native beliefs

Important Festivals   Christmas, Easter, Farmers' Day, Idd-El-Fitr, Idd-El-Hajj, Independence Day, Mwalimu Nyerere Day, Saba Saba, Union Day, Zanzibar Revolution Day

Currency   Tanzanian shilling (1,061 TZS = U.S. $1 in 2004)

Opposite: Bao is a popular leisure activity among Tanzanians.

Glossary

ancestors: family members from the past, farther back than grandparents.

appeal: the bringing of a legal case to a higher court to be heard over again.

cassavas: roots eaten in many ways.

conservation: the protection and careful use of natural resources.

constitution: a set of citizen rights and laws for a country's government.

cultural: relating to the customs, beliefs, laws, and ways of living of a people.

democracy: a government in which the citizens elect their leaders by vote.

descendants: people born in a recent generation to one group or family.

ethnic: relating to a race or culture that has similar customs and languages.

executive: relating to the branch of the government that puts laws into effect.

exported (v): sold and shipped products from one country to another country.

fertile: able to feed or produce life.

mainland: a continent or large piece of land, as opposed to an island.

missions: places set up by people who come to a country to do good works.

native: belonging to a land or region by having first grown or been born there.

parliament: elected government group that makes the laws for their country.

pilgrimages: journeys made to a holy place as an act of religious devotion.

plateau: a wide, flat area of land that is surrounded by lower land.

Ramadan: the Islamic holy month. All healthy Muslims must not eat or drink from dawn to dusk during the month.

savannas: dry grasslands.

sorghum: a type of tropical grass that produces grain.

sultan: a king, usually of a Muslim land.

traditional: relating to customs or styles passed down through the generations.

tribute: money paid to another nation to ensure peace or to gain protection.

tropical: very warm and wet.

United Nations: an international group that promotes understanding and peace and helps nations develop.

vocational: related to a job or profession.

warlord: a military leader, usually a person who rules by using force.

More Books to Read

Cheetah. Taylor Morrison (Henry Holt and Company)

Clever Tortoise: A Traditional African Tale. Francesca Martin (Candlewick Press)

The Crocodile Family Book. Mark Deeble (North-South Books)

Into Wild Tanzania. The Jeff Corwin Experience series. John Woodward & Jeff Corwin (Blackbirch Press)

The Maasai of East Africa. Jamie Hetfield (PowerKids Press)

Subira Subira. Tololwa M. Mollel (Clarion Books)

Tanzania. Africa series. Joan Vos MacDonald (Mason Crest Publishers)

Tanzania: Through the Eyes of a Child. Connie Bickman (Abdo & Daughters Publishing)

With Love. Jane Goodall (North-South Books)

Zebras. All about Wild Animals series. (Gareth Stevens)

Videos

Africa Close-Up: Egypt & Tanzania. Children of the Earth series (Maryknoll World Productions)

Biomes for Students: Grasslands (SVE and Discovery Channel School)

East Africa: Worlds Together for Kids series (Elmer Hawkes)

World's Last Great Places: Tanzania— Thorn Tree Country (National Geographic Video)

Web Sites

www.altrec.com/features/crownofafrica/

www.factmonster.com/ipka/ A0108028.html

www.pbs.org/wnet/nature/serengeti/

www.serengeti.org/

Due to the dynamic nature of the Internet, some web sites stay current longer than others. To find additional web sites, use a reliable search engine with one or more of the following keywords to help you locate information about Tanzania. Keywords: *Dar es Salaam, Mount Kilimanjaro, Serengeti, tanzanite, Zanzibar*.

Index